THE GLASS TOWER

FAIRY TALES REDUX SERIES

BOOK 1

I0521451

BY EMILY GRAY

THE GLASS TOWER

First Edition. May 6, 2021.
Copyright © 2021 Emily Gray.
ISBN 978-0-9988684-7-9

Published by Fantastic Optimism Publishing 2021

Cover Design © Matt Billingsley
Cover Image © Berti Weber from Pexels.com

Dedication

For anyone who ever needed a fairy tale,

Believe

Description

Zel Thatcher, imprisoned in a glass tower high-rise, covets the day he can escape his tyrannical uncle. With only music to keep him company, he's lost the passion he once possessed… until a dark-haired beauty restores his soul's melody with her own and proves she might be the one to save him.

Regina Prince, born into music royalty, performs by choice rather than necessity. Her free-spirit brings her to Corona, where hearing an exquisite performance inspires her to find its source. She never imagines she'll discover someone whose heart sings like hers.

Will Zel's uncle destroy their happily ever after?

Chapter 1

"Standing there to stare out the window is pointless."

My back stiffens at my uncle's commanding tone.

On the other side of the glass, the vast City of Corona spreads out below as I gaze over rooftops from stories above them. It's a scene I look at daily, longing to know what it's like to experience the beautiful city's sights, sounds, and smells. Instead, I'm stuck in this high-rise, isolated from everything. It's an asylum for my safety. At least that's what my uncle has told me for most of my life. But for me, this tower is more like a prison, one I desperately want to escape.

Without turning to acknowledge him, I snap back. "Considering it's the only way I can see the city, I'll have to disagree."

"It's for your protection you stay here, Zel. You'd do well to remember that."

The words may be spoken to sound like he's concerned, however, the bite in his tone paint a different picture.

"How is *this* protection? Being shut off from everything and everyone?"

"The world is a terrible place. Your parents knew that. There are plenty of people who would take advantage of you because of them. You learned that the hard way once before. Remember? You're safer here."

Turning to face him, a familiar white hot anger sizzles under my skin from this ongoing argument. I'm honestly surprised I've lasted this long under his thumb. My patience wears thinner each time we go around this carousel. The only reason I can give for my suitable behavior is because he's the only family I have after my parents' deaths a decade ago. And yet, the contempt I have for the man in front of me has outweighed any respect taught to me. My frustration compounds because he's also my only means of financial support. A reality he feels is necessary to point out to me often.

"Being locked away here wasn't my idea," I growl. "As I recall, you didn't even consider my opinion on the subject."

"Because your opinion doesn't matter. You're a *child*." He sneers the word as if it's the equivalent to gum on the bottom of his shoe.

"No, Uncle, I'm not. Not anymore."

With my twenty-first birthday fast approaching, I'm finding I can no longer be blindly obedient. The desire to live life on my terms has reached its peak, regardless of any risk or cost.

"You *will* do what I say is necessary. It is not negotiable," he thunders.

He punctuates his statement by turning on his heel and leaving the penthouse, the heavy door slamming behind him.

As irritation races through my veins, I turn back to the glass with my fists tight and jaw clenched. The only thing I wish for is a way to break free from my tower of solitude.

I've been in isolation for almost half of my life. When I was younger and put in my uncle's care, he wanted nothing to do with me. A bachelor and childless, I merely became an obligation rather than what I should have been, the son of a beloved younger sister. He shipped me away quickly to attend the most elite boarding school. I guess he thought it would protect me, along with keeping me out of his hair.

But it soon became apparent I wasn't like the other students. They knew it and so did I, which meant I had no genuine friends. Being the son of prominent parents didn't help matters either. I had no connections, except to my music. It was my constant companion, much the same as it is now.

Once I resigned myself to being alone, I focused on my talent and flourished. My teachers recognized my potential, but others saw an opportunity for extortion and deceit. My family's name, including mine, was used to gain the school and its administrators recognition and access to significant financial backing. Not long after that, my uncle threatened legal action and pulled me out of the school.

I was brought back to live with my uncle, who hired private tutors for my studies while he kept a watchful eye over me. He never allowed me to leave the captivity of our penthouse. At first, I appreciated the bubble of security. Being young and sheltered, I hadn't known people could be so ruthless and devious. Nevertheless, it didn't take long before I felt smothered and hidden. Whenever I felt restless though, he would remind me it was for my safety by recounting the manipulations to which others had subjected me.

As I grew older and my talent exceeded the expectations and capabilities of my mentors, my uncle fired them one after another. Then, he simply stop employing anyone altogether. This isolated me even more. Confinement became desolate. His treatment of me also turned cruel and belligerent, losing all pretenses of decency.

Now, I long for a day when I can leave this prison, live the life I want, and be free from his control once and for all.

Feeling defeated once again, I lean forward and place my forehead against the window. The chill of the glass soothes the dull ache in my head. I close my eyes to imagine what it might be like to stroll along the streets or even through the park as a regular person. It's something I haven't experienced in longer than I can remember. The scene outside is nothing more than a moving picture to me. It might as well be on a television screen. I begin to wonder if it might even be a part of my imagination.

As I heave a sigh, my eyelids open to a sudden flash of color on the sidewalk. The vibrancy and swift motion are a shock to my overwhelmed system. It seems out of place in the daily humdrum of the city.

Quick to grab the binoculars on the stand beside me, I adjust the dials to focus. I search and find a girl with waves of shimmering brown hair standing outside the building.

I watch as she lifts two bright, rope-handled bags from the cab parked at the curb. She places them behind her with what looks like a suitcase, a guitar case, and a small box already on the sidewalk. She leans in the front window to pay for her fare. Her lips move as she speaks to the driver and then her face breaks into a wide smile. She stands to watch as the cab pulls away and gives a brief wave.

After turning to face the front entrance, she's poised with her hands on her hips.

I can't help noticing the generous curves of her body.

Moving the focus back on her face, I see the corners of her lips lift as she looks up the height of the building. She takes her time while she looks up like she's studying the structure or admiring a piece of art. She seems to be oblivious to the people and the chaos of the city going on around her, content in her own little world.

I see her gaze shift back down. Her lips move as she smiles sweetly at someone. Her expression is open and welcoming. I'm suddenly envious of whoever is on the receiving end of her attention.

Angling the binoculars, I notice the doorman walking toward her. He bends to grab the box, suitcase, and bags. She waves him away from the guitar and gently picks it up herself. She holds it close to her as if it's the most important possession to her. I can understand the sentiment.

Before she moves forward, she pauses one more time, looking up. My stare remains focused on her while I hold my breath. I pause and wait to see what she'll do. I wonder if she can see me, which is silly considering I'm ten stories above her.

As I berate myself for the foolishness, I begin to lower the binoculars. In the last moment, her gaze swings directly to me. I'm instantly mesmerized by a pair of crystal blue eyes, framed with long, dark lashes. I'm frozen in place. My lungs burn with the need to exhale.

Several seconds pass. With a hundred feet separating us, I feel a magnetic pull. After several more breaths, her face breaks into the most extraordinary smile I've ever seen. My heart thumps like a bass drum inside my chest.

Shock pushes me back from the window while my arms lower the lenses from my eyes. I feel as though my world has just turned upside down.

Chapter 2

I've watched out the window every day for a week, hoping to catch some glimpse of the girl with the bright colors. I've failed to spot her even once. The loss has left me in a melancholy mood and irritated.

Maybe she was just a figment of my imagination. At least that's what I keep trying to convince myself.

Sitting at the piano, I feel agitated and unfulfilled.

I've spent the last fifteen years finding solace in the black and white keys and the music I play. But now, nothing soothes the discontent inside me.

Practicing has become a chore, instead of a haven. The notes are sharp to my senses, almost stinging with each measure. The music that streams from the instrument is chaotic and somber. I can remember only one other time this sound poured from my fingertips. And then, I had just lost my parents.

Hearing punctuated footsteps on the tile floor, my body stiffens. The last thing I need right now is another confrontation with him. My uncle is seldom a source of anything other than frustration, especially these days.

"Zel, you have a recording session tomorrow morning. I expect you to be there. And play something more enjoyable."

His sneer sets my teeth on edge.

"What does it matter what I play?"

"It's called marketing appeal and excellent business strategy. I doubt anyone will want to listen to the dribble I've been hearing from you the last few days."

"I play what I feel."

"Well, feel something else," he clips. "Your appointment time is nine."

I am thoroughly dismissed once again as he turns on his heel and leaves the penthouse without a backward glance.

My frustration boils over and comes out in a vicious cacophony. The sound reverberates through the surrounding room. As I pour all my tension into the notes, the release helps express how I feel. I have no other outlet, and thankfully, the piano is a forgiving instrument as I punish the keys. I finish the piece with a dramatic, vigorous chord. My fingers ache from the force exerted into the notes, but at least my emotions are calmer.

Rising from the bench, I move to the window again. I feel the outside pulling me to be free more every day, whispering for me to find an escape. If I had any means of supporting myself, I would have left this prison a long time ago. Unfortunately, I have no money of my own. All of it belongs to my uncle. I wouldn't even know where to begin or how to survive on my own, but my frustration has pushed me past the point of being afraid to take the risk.

As I rest my forehead on folded hands pressing to the glass, I stare at the street below me. I'm high enough that faces are obscure, but hues and movement fill the sidewalk.

I don't know how long I'm standing there when I see a familiar burst of color. It's like the sun exploding on the horizon and steals my breath.

Reaching for the binoculars again, I focus on my mystery girl. I don't stop to analyze the fact that I've already laid claim to a girl I've never met and only seen twice. But regardless, everything in me gravitates to her, craving a connection.

My gaze follows the bounce of her hair and her graceful steps as she exits the building, then waits at the curb. She fiddles with her phone as her head dips slightly up and down and her body sways. Again, she seems immersed in what she's doing, paying no attention to anything else around her. By the movement of her body, she must have music playing. The thought makes me smile.

A cab approaches a moment later, prompting her to look up from her screen. The doorman opens the back passenger door. She climbs in and offers him a smile of thanks.

After she shuts the door, she rolls down the window and allows her head to ease through the opening. When the car pulls away, she tips her head to look up the building as she did the first day I saw her.

Through the lenses, our gazes connect. The smile on her face widens. And once again, I'm a slave to whatever power she possesses.

I spend the rest of my afternoon playing. But this time, the music flows from my fingers with ease. Each note is light and stirring, filled with euphoria.

Chapter 3

I spend the next morning in the confines of a recording booth with a piano and too many microphones surrounding me. The space is a converted apartment that occupies the same level as the penthouse. I don't even have the luxury of stepping outside to feel the sun on my face to get to it. The fact just reinforces how much of a prison my home is.

There is a one-way mirror a sound producer and my uncle stand behind while I play a repertoire of pieces. I play for several hours. The pieces I select are bright, quick-paced, and cheery. Even my uncle's perpetual sourness can't take away from my excellent mood.

We finish at the studio and then I'm sent straight back to my tower confinement. My uncle mumbles something about having several meetings scheduled and not to expect him back for dinner before he leaves me alone again. The reprieve is fine by me, honestly. The thought of sitting across the table from him while trying to choke down food is an exercise in patience I'd rather avoid.

Knowing I have the apartment to myself allows me to relax. It also gives me the opportunity to play pieces my uncle would never approve of, ever. They're outside the norm of what other musicians consider classical, but I love them. I found the sheet music tucked away in a tattered box of my mother's belongings years ago. The pages arefilled with her beautiful script while the tune reminds me of her sweet, melodic voice. They are the most precious things I own.

I haven't been able to play the pieces often. But, when I do, they help me feel closer to her, a feeling I hold on to and cherish.

After playing through three of the pieces, there is a light sound at the door. I pause from the music to be sure I've heard correctly. No one ever knocks on the main door. Any maintenance people would use the service elevator. Plus, my uncle would be here if he expected anyone and stays until they leave.

Just as my fingers settle on the keys again, a soft, firm knock lands on the hard mahogany. I'm so stunned by the rare sound I take a moment before I move across the room to open the entrance. As the door swings inward, standing before me is a vision in a radiant yellow dress, my mystery girl.

She is beyond breathtaking. Petite in her frame with porcelain skin, she stands with a bright smile, warm brown eyes staring at me. Every nerve in my body is suddenly on high alert and buzzing across my skin.

Clearing the rough sandpaper in my throat, I can only strangle out one word. "Yes?"

"Hi! I'm so sorry for disturbing you."

"It's fine. Can I help you with something?" I pray my voice hasn't wavered and revealed the butterflies in my stomach.

"Well, not really, I guess. It's just that I heard the most wonderful music while I was in the elevator. I've been on a mission searching the building to figure out who was responsible."

"It was me."

I cringe. My answer sounds foolish to my ears. If the girl agrees, she doesn't give any sign.

"Yay, mystery solved then! I have to say it was truly beautiful."

"Um, thank you." Her compliment has me standing a little taller.

"Well," she pauses, as if waiting for something. "I just wanted to figure that out."

She seems hesitant to leave. She shifts on her feet before she turns toward the elevator. The realization that I need her to stay slams into me. It seems impossible to let her walk away when I have her standing on my doorstep right in front of me this very moment. Even though my uncle never allows visitors, I can't risk throwing away this chance to be near her, to talk to her.

Despite knowing his rules, I ask, "May I invite you in?" Then, wanting to use a bit of persuasion, I add, "I'm not quite done practicing. You could listen, if you like."

Her smile transforms from sweet and shy to brilliant. "Really? Thank you."

As she moves over the threshold, her shoulder brushes my shirt. Sparks shoot across my chest as a light scent of roses wafts around us. It's soft and sweet, tickling my nose. The fragrance brings an immediate layer of calm over me, but turns my senses hyperactive. I am keenly aware of her in my space.

I watch as she enters the expansive living room, making her way to the black grand piano that dominates the area by the floor to ceiling windows. It's like she's a moth drawn to a flame. Her hand glides over the glossy lid with slow, reverent strokes.

"This is an exquisite instrument."

"Thank you. Do you play?"

She laughs a bright tone that flows through the void of my prison, filling every corner.

"Oh, no, not the piano. Too complicated for me," she murmurs.

"But, you *do* play music. The guitar, maybe?"

Her gaze flashes to me, her eyes wide, but there is more knowing in her stare than surprise.

I realize I've given myself away somewhat and shift uncomfortably on my feet.

"I do. And you would know that how?" she teases. "I don't think I've seen you around the building before."

"Well, um, I don't get out much. But, I look around the city," I say as I gesture to the binoculars hung securely on their stand. "I saw you arriving outside the building about a week ago. You looked like you were carrying a guitar." I shrug one shoulder as my eyes dip to the floor, nervousness flowing through me at her reaction.

"Oh, right. Yeah, I just moved into the building that day."

Afraid of what she'll think of me, I stammer, "I'm not some creepy stalker or something, I swear."

With a smile, she says, "That's good to know, but I didn't think you were. I'm Gina."

Her eyes crinkled at the sides and sparkle when she looks at me.

"I'm Zel."

"That's an unusual name. I like it. It's nice to meet you."

"Likewise."

I pause, not knowing what else to say.

"Where should I sit?" she asks as she looks around the room. "I don't want to distract you."

Little does she know it doesn't matter where she sits. I'll be aware of her no matter what. I'm certain it'll be the first time since I started playing the music doesn't surround me within its cocoon.

"Wherever is comfortable for you," I tell her.

She crosses to the cream-colored settee. Folding her legs beneath her, she settles herself in a graceful, fluid motion. In her bright, yellow dress, she looks like live art as she places her hands in her lap and then waits.

Walking to the piano, I feel her eyes on me. I decide not to use any sheet music and play from memory. I don't think I could concentrate on following the lines of notes, anyway.

I lower myself onto the bench, breathing deeply. Placing my fingers on the keys, I close my eyes. To my surprise, instead of feeling nervous to be in front of someone, the thought of Gina watching fuels my desire to play.

Notes flow out of me with a level of passion I haven't felt before now. Music has always been my safe place, but lately, it's become more of an escape from everything I don't know how to face. Right now though, it's become an awakening. I'm lost in the music. My blood sings through my veins as my fingertips float across the keys.

I hit the last note, slowly opening my eyes as the echoing sound fades from the air.

"Wow," she gasps softly.

I had nearly forgotten Gina sat there, except for the infusion of feeling her presence evoked.

I slide to the end of the bench to face her. Her face has a slight flush to it and her eyes sparkle.

"Zel, that was amazing."

Elated by her praise, I reply, "Thank you."

She rises from the couch, brushing her hands down her skirt to straighten it.

"Well, I should be going. I've intruded on you enough. Thank you for letting me stay and listen."

Gina begins the walk to the door. A panic erupts in my belly, but I have no idea what to say to convince her to stay a little while longer. I cross the room to stand beside her, trying to hold on to every moment she's still here.

As she pushes the lever to open the door, she turns back to me.

"I know this is forward of me, but can I come back to listen again?"

"Of course." I'm ready to jump out of my skin in the rush to say yes.

The beautiful smile I'm rewarded with makes me feel relieved. I know I'll have the chance to see her again. It also ignites a layer of anticipation for the next time.

"Bye, Zel. I'll see you soon."

"I look forward to it, Gina."

She slips through the opening in the hallway.

As the latch clicks softly in place, I stand there wondering if I've just met an angel.

Chapter 4

My uncle returns home later that evening. As usual, he retreats to his office. He barely acknowledges me, which is fine by me.

I keep to myself, eat dinner, and call it a night early by going to bed.

As I lay there, an image of Gina comes to mind. The memory of her fragrance and voice wash over me. A thrill shoots through me at what she'd feel like in my arms. I wonder if I'll have the chance to find out when I see her again. I hated to see her leave, but I like that she said she'll come back.

Just as I doze off to sleep, a shadow looms in my bedroom doorway. My uncle's furious voice startles me.

"You would do well to remember my rules, Zel."

Not feeling inclined to cower and irritated by his intrusion, I snap back, "And what rule have I forgotten this time, Uncle?"

His words boom through the air. "The rule where visitors are forbidden. I saw her. Who was she?"

I'm stunned into silence. It's hard to imagine how he knew Gina had been here. I decide it's best to be careful about how much I divulge. I sit up in the bed to buy myself a few moments before I answer.

"I don't know. Just some girl that knocked on the door." I hope my tone appears nonchalant and gives nothing away of my genuine feelings about her.

"You don't know, and yet you invited her in? Into *my* home?" he snarls.

I realize the only way for him to know about the visit is somehow to have seen her here. My mind turns over all the possibilities. The one that makes the most sense is there must be a camera around the front door as part of the security system.

My eyes adjust to the darkness of the room with the moon providing the only source of light. My uncle's form hills the doorway, feet braced shoulder width apart and arms crossed over his chest. I can tell by his stance, his level of anger increases the longer he has to wait for my answer. I decide it might be best not to provoke him further and give a reply I hope satisfies him. Thankful he can't see me very well in the dim light, I try to maintain an air of indifference in my voice.

"She heard me playing from the elevator. I just let her listen to me practice. Nothing more." The lie falls easily from my lips, despite the racing of my pulse.

"It was hours before she left. I won't tolerate that kind of disregard."

His statement confirms my theory about the camera, but I wonder if there is more to the system. I test him even though I know it's a risk.

"I doubt she'll return. She mentioned something about being on vacation and leaving soon."

"All the better. She would be a distraction. One you can't afford."

The response gives me all the information I need. But, then I think about the sudden change of his argument. It throws me off balance and sounds more alarms in my head. Over the years, I've thought he was keeping things hidden from me. Now, I'm certain of it. The urge to push him into a corner for the truth has me determined to challenge him.

"A distraction from what exactly? All I do is eat, sleep, and play my music." I pause in frustration. "There aren't even any tutors or lessons anymore, nothing else to occupy my time. You've cut everything else out of my life. And I thought the problem was about following your rules, anyway?"

"It's for your own good. Your focus must be on your music."

"Why? What kind of existence is that for me?"

"It's one that keeps you safe."

"From what? Why won't you tell me anything more than that?" I plead.

"I have warned you about how deceptive people are. Everyone is out for themselves. You being here is for your own protection."

Aggravation boils inside me. I'm done with this constant state of isolation.

"Does that include you?" The words are out before I think to stop them.

He forces a heavy breath through his nose before his voice thunders, "She is not to step another foot in this penthouse again. Nor is anyone else." Once he dictates his order, he abruptly turns on his heel, slams the bedroom door, and leaves.

A steady simmer of bitterness flows through me. The years I've spent following his rules and not asking questions are quickly ending. The man is my family, my mother's older brother, her only sibling, and should feel some affinity for me. But, he doesn't, and never has. Not since the day I came to live with him has he showed me even an ounce of affection as his nephew. He barely acknowledges my existence most days, which leads me to wonder why he has kept me with him.

I go to sleep thinking about the decision I should have made so long ago. It's time to take a chance and figure out how to survive on my own, out from under my oppressive uncle.

Chapter 5

After a silent, tension-filled breakfast at the table the next day, my uncle left without a word. I can't say I'm disappointed in his lack of interaction with me.

His absence today has allowed me to consider the thoughts that swirled in my head last night. Because of them, my morning practice is much more subdued and introspective than usual. Notes ring out from the piano as my fingers run over the keys on autopilot. Having so many songs memorized in my head is a benefit of playing for most of my life.

By mid-morning, my fingers ache. As I'm about to stop for a break, a familiar knock lands on the door.

Excitement drums through me, but then it's followed by concern of what might happen if my uncle finds out she's here again. Disappointment consumes me when I realize I can't let Gina in the apartment.

I open the door to her angelic face. All thoughts of my uncle and his rules evaporate for a moment.

"Hi," she murmurs, a sweet, singular word sets my heart to an erratic beat.

"Um, hey." I stall. My mind races to find a way for her to stay.

"Zel, what's wrong?"

Unable to come up with a solution, I sigh. I decide it's better to tell her the unpleasant news.

"I'm afraid I can't invite you in today, Gina."

"Oh." Her crestfallen expression splinters through my heart.

"It's not because I don't want to. I do, but my uncle found out you were here yesterday. He has strict rules about visitors. Actually, he has strict rules about everything. I shouldn't have let you in. I'm sorry."

"Did you get in trouble? I hope not on account of me."

"No, not really. It definitely could have been worse. Just a bunch of him blustering hot air. At least this time."

She tilts her head for a moment, considering.

"How did he know I was here?"

"My guess? He has a camera here at the entrance somewhere. It wouldn't surprise me, really. I know there's an expensive security system for the penthouse. I just never knew how much was involved with it until last night. It's crazy he would watch whoever comes and goes from this place."

"That sounds really over the top, maybe even paranoid. Is there a microphone for him to hear things, too, do you think?" she chuckles after her words, not really understanding how my uncle is about things.

"Yeah, well, you've never met my uncle." My cheeks heat with equal parts of aggravation and embarrassment. "From what I can tell though, there's no audio recording."

"Wow, I was kind of joking. I'm sorry. He seems like a tough pill to swallow."

"He is. You have no idea how much."

"Well, I don't want to cause you any trouble with your uncle. Although, I was looking forward to hearing you play some more," she tells me with a smile. The impact hits me in the center of my chest.

The last thing I want is for her to leave. Wracking my brain, I try to think of a way to have her stay without my uncle knowing. Then, it hits me.

"The service elevator!"

"Excuse me?"

"There's a service elevator coming up to the apartment at the back. My uncle always has maintenance people use it. He doesn't want them coming in through the front with equipment."

"Oh, right! That must be the same one the movers used when I moved in. Do you think there's a camera like on this door?"

"There might not be. He's always here whenever some kind of work is scheduled. And he won't leave people here alone. He stays until everything is completed. Otherwise, why would he do that? I can't believe I didn't think of it sooner."

"That sounds reasonable, I guess. But, I really don't want to be responsible for him being angry with you if he were to find out again."

Feeling fed up with his treatment, I admit, "He's always angry. It's nothing new. Besides, having you here would be worth it. I'd like you to stay."

"I'd like that, too." As her smile blooms, a beautiful blush covers her cheeks.

A frown pulls at my brows. "But, there's one problem."

"What's that?"

"I don't know if there's anything special like a key or code needed to use it."

"Don't worry. I know what to do. I saw how the movers used it when they brought my furniture. The elevator only moves to the apartment number punched in, nowhere else. I remember one man grumbling about it when they got the number wrong."

"Okay, that works. The entry is right outside the kitchen."

She nods, and then makes her way across the hall to push the elevator button.

"Gina?" She turns as I call her. "It might be better if there's no one around when you come up."

"I'll make sure no one sees me. Be right back." Her expression is serious, but she winks letting me know she's on board with our Cloak and Dagger plan.

I wait anxiously for her return, pacing the kitchen. It feels like an eternity before I hear the soft bell of the elevator.

Striding to the kitchen door, I open it right as she steps off into the hallway. We were just together a moment ago, but seeing her now hits me full force, knocking the air from my lungs.

Gina rushes forward wrapping her arms around my waist, clinging to me, and buries her face in my shirt. Her ear is directly over my thudding heartbeat. Automatically, I fold myself around her. My arms tighten to hold her close.

I don't understand what's happening between us. It seems so crazy. We've only just met. All I know is there was an emptiness I felt inside before I met her. I've felt it when she's gone, too. But, now that she's here, I feel whole for the first time in years.

Chapter 6

Gina and I have spent the last two weeks meeting in secret. They have been the best two weeks of my life.

She comes every day around mid-morning once my uncle has left. Then, with a lot of reluctance, departs before dinner to avoid being caught. If my uncle suspects anything or wonders about my change in mood, he says nothing.

Despite the niggling fear in the pit of my stomach he'll find out, I can't tell Gina to stay away. She has become the air that I breathe. I think I might be the same for her. At least that's what I hope.

The thing I fear though is the feeling of change I know is coming. My twenty-first birthday approaches in less than a week. The time draws near for me to break free from my uncle.

Gina arrives for the day, looking vibrant in yellow. Her hair bounces across her shoulders in a high ponytail. Her eyes are bright and carry a hint of mischief in them as does her smile. I wonder what she has planned for us.

As she makes her way to me, she rises on her tiptoes and kisses my cheek. The skin tingles where her lips briefly pressed. A light flush spreads over her face.

"Hey," she says shyly.

"Hi, beautiful." My compliment deepens her color and causes her to duck her head. I kiss her forehead and tease, "What do you have going on in that head of yours?"

Bringing her gaze up, her eyes dance with merriment.

"I thought we could do something different today."

"Oh? What's that?"

"What if we went outside? I have somewhere I want to show you. I know you'll love it," she hedges.

She knows I've been a prisoner in this high-rise apartment since leaving boarding school. I don't leave the confines of these glass walls, except for when I go to the recording studio down the hall.

"I don't know."

Escaping, if only temporarily, tempts me, but it's a huge risk. An excitement buzzes under my skin and speeds up my heartbeat. Yet, I'm still hesitant. Gina picks up on my distress.

"I know you're worried about your uncle. But, think about it. I've been coming to see you for weeks and nothing. He hasn't said a word to you about anything. If we leave out of the service elevator and aren't gone too long, we'll be fine."

I consider the possibility of being caught. My reluctance to follow the rules grows in strength each time I see her. She's right that nothing has happened since she started using the service elevator. My uncle hasn't even mentioned her again.

"We'll watch the time, I promise." Her eyes plead with me, wanting the chance to show me a freedom I've rarely experienced, the one I crave almost constantly now since meeting her.

Enticed by the opportunity to make her happy, and maybe by the risk, I agree.

Pulling me onto the elevator in a flurry, she pushes the button for the lobby.

"How are we supposed to get by the front desk without being seen?" I'm actually tempted to walk right by without a care, but I'm not at the point where my uncle's reaction isn't a concern anymore.

"Leave that to me," she says with a wink. At the opening of the doors, she says, "Wait at the corner until you know it's clear."

"How will I know?"

"You'll know." She grins.

Gina scoots out of the elevator. I hear her with an animated tone tell the front desk attendant, "Oh my goodness! Can you help me? I've lost my earring by the elevators. I heard it drop and can't find it."

"Miss, I'm not supposed to leave my position," he informs her.

"Please," she begs. "You don't understand. They were my grandmother's. They are so important to me. They're all I have left of her." The dramatic agony she infuses into her words is flawless. She could win an award for her performance. I can only imagine the tortured expression on her face.

"Yes, fine. But, only for a minute," the clerk sighs.

Peering around the corner, I see Gina steer the guard to the opposite side of the lobby.

"It must have fallen right over here somewhere when I came in the building." She points to the floor, making sure the man's back is to me.

Once he is on his hands and knees, engrossed in the search for an imaginary earring, she waves her hand behind her back. That's when I make a break for it.

I bolt from my hiding place, move across the open lobby with hurried, quiet steps, and out the revolving door. Before it pushes me to the outside, I hear her exclaim that she found it and thanking him profusely for his help. A few moments later, she skips out of the building, looking up and down the street for me.

I'm leaning against the side of the structure, watching her with amusement. I whistle lightly, a crisp, clean sound. Gina's head spins toward me. She giggles exuberantly and rushes to where I'm standing. Her delight is contagious. A laugh bubbles from my throat as she entwines her fingers with mine, then pulls me down the sidewalk. I haven't ever felt this free.

"Come on!"

"Where are we going?"

"You'll see." Her beautiful eyes sparkle in the sunlight with glee.

We move through the streets of Corona, soaking up the sights and sounds of the city. In the distance, I see glittering water and an expanse of green. As we approach, birds flock to the edge of the rich marsh, while others glide over the mirror surface of the lake. I stand awestruck at the beauty and the music of nature all around us.

"Do you like it?" she whispers.

Rendered speechless, I take a moment to find my voice and the words for the beauty I see.

"I haven't seen anything so lovely in quite a while." I turn my gaze away from the scene to look at her. "Except for the first time when I saw you and every day since," I add.

A crimson flush hits her cheeks full force. She hides her face, leaning it against my upper arm. I kiss the top of her head before returning to admire the landscape. The sigh I release is born of contentment and hope.

Chapter 7

We spend some time walking hand in hand around the lake. I soak in the sunshine, feeling at peace and alive.

Even though we haven't been away from the penthouse for very long, the time has been extraordinary. The bad part is I know we need to make our way back to the building. After this taste of freedom, I'm reluctant to return.

As we near the tower, a sign catches my eye, an advertisement showcasing a musician. In bold, golden script letters, my name spans across the top with music symbols and a picture of a gleaming piano on it. My feet halt beneath me from the shock coursing through my body. My sudden stop jars Gina's arm, making her steps falter.

"Zel, what is it?" She looks around nervously for some explanation.

All I can do is stare at the image, unanswered questions and puzzle pieces floating through my mind.

I've suspected my uncle used the time I spent in the recording studio for some business venture. I'm not an idiot. But, I had no proof or any idea the magnitude to which all my efforts grew. Apparently, I've been kept in the dark far longer than I imagined. He's used me for a much greater benefit to himself. The worst part is being taken advantage of by the person who should care for me. The thought sets my blood to boiling.

Without a word, I turn to head back to the building, not knowing what else to do. The urge to confront my uncle is almost overwhelming.

My long strides make it difficult for Gina to keep up. She hurries to stay by my side. The tension in the air between us is heavy with unspoken questions. Entering the elevator makes it almost suffocating.

When we exit into the hallway, Gina finally speaks again.

"Zel, talk to me, please."

I can't help wondering about her lack of surprise at seeing the sign. For her, it seemed like an everyday occurrence, which it might likely be.

Barely able to control my frustration, I ground out, "Have you known who I am all this time?"

"Of course," she says.

"And?"

"And what?" she shrugs.

"You've never thought to mention it or the fact that other people know who I am as well?"

"Because it doesn't matter."

All the air leaves my lungs, turning my anger into a sour queasiness in my belly. Her words strike hard, slicing quick and deep. Forcing clenched hands into my pockets, my stare finds the tile floor. My heartbeat thumps in my ears.

"Oh, well..." My voice fades as words fail me. It's suddenly painfully clear whatever I thought Gina and I have is only one-sided. My side.

Maybe she's just like everyone else my uncle has always preached about who take advantage of others for their own benefit. And now, it seems he falls into that category as well. The knowledge spreads like ice freezing my heart.

A faint shuffling sound whispers through the room as I struggle to breathe.

Warmth spreads across my skin when Gina's soft hands frame my face. Lifting my gaze to her eyes, I see a small smile play on her lips.

"Zel, I know who you are to the outside world. I have known since you opened the door when I knocked that first day. That doesn't matter to me. What does is the person I know from being with you."

Her words filter into my ears. When my mind finally catches up to what she's said, joy spreads through me like wildfire. The smile on my face forms from pure exhilaration.

Unable to stop myself, my arms encircle her waist and swing her around into the air. Her bell-like squeal rings out as we spin. We make three turns before I set her to her feet again.

My heart thuds and my chest heaves. Laughter spills from me. This is the happiest I've felt in my entire life.

Gina's eyes sparkle with delight. Her cheeks are flushed. The buzz of electricity flows through us both, keeping me connected to her.

With my hands still at her waist, and her fingers gripping my forearms, my lips crush onto hers. I swallow her surprise as her body melts into mine. One of my arms spans her lower back, anchoring her to me. The other travels up between her shoulder blades and up to her neck. My fingers tangle into her hair to hold her steady as my mouth devours her. Her whimper fuels my need for her. Moments pass before reality awakens me from the dream I'm experiencing.

With self-control I didn't know I could summon, I slowly pull away. But, Gina doesn't let me retreat. Her lips follow me, chasing to keep us melded together. Her tongue traces my bottom lip, teasing me.

I part my lips slightly, giving her control. She takes advantage immediately. Her fingers tunnel through my hair while she plunges her tongue into my mouth. The groan I release vibrates through my ribs.

She breaks the kiss with a smile as we both gasp for breath.

"I've wanted to do that for so long, Zel."

"Me, too," I admit. "I wish you could stay."

"Maybe soon."

"I'm not sure how that'll be possible with my uncle."

"Things have a way of working out. You'll see."

The certainty in her voice gives me no other choice than to believe her. From the moment I met her, everything I believed to be possible has changed.

Unable to stop myself, my lips find hers again. I pour all of my desire into a last kiss.

Gina grips the front of my shirt, seemingly torn between pulling me closer and breaking us apart. Finally, our mouths separate.

"I should go," she whispers.

"I know. But, I don't want you to."

"I'll be back tomorrow."

"I'm counting on it, Gina."

"Nothing could keep me away, Zel."

Rising on her tiptoes, she brushes our lips together one last time before backing into the elevator. Her smile is the most beautiful thing about her. It's the last image I see before the metal doors slide closed.

Chapter 8

I pace the length of the elevator hallway the next day, surprised I don't wear a permanent path into the marble floor. I've been expecting Gina's arrival since my uncle left the penthouse with bags packed early this morning.

The evening after my date in the park with Gina, he informed me at dinner he'd be gone for the weekend. While the prospect of having the empty apartment and time with Gina thrilled me, my uncle's dismissal of my birthday still burned.

It's not like I expect him to throw me a party. Our relationship is nonexistent and I know almost no one else who might come to a celebration. But, a slight part of me would have liked for him to at least acknowledge it. Perhaps even care enough to stick around and show me some kind of family loyalty. I suppose it was one last hope I had.

Instead of dwelling on the broken relationship with my uncle though, I'm focusing on my impatience not turning me inside out. The wait for Gina is torture. Knowing we'll have extended, uninterrupted time together sets my blood buzzing through my veins. To hold her in my arms and possibly in my bed might be the best birthday present I could ever receive. I just hope she feels the same.

The elevator bell chimes, setting loose the butterflies in my stomach. As the doors open, my breath catches in my throat at the vision before me.

Gina exits the steel box like she's stepping out of a painting. Clothed in a deep purple dress, she is the epitome of regality. Her shoulders and arms are bare, showcasing her flawless, porcelain skin. Soft tendrils of her hair fall around her lovely face. And her smile is a beam of pure joy. Nothing can compare to her beauty in this moment.

I barely hear the light clicking of her shoes over the thud of my heart in my ears as she walks toward me.

She pulls a small box from behind her back, handing it to me.

"Happy birthday, Zel."

"What's this?"

She shrugs innocently, then blushes. "Everyone needs a birthday cake."

Opening the lid, I see a decadent chocolate cupcake topped with a red candy heart.

Warmth spreads through me at the thoughtful gesture. It's been so long since anyone did anything for me.

Leaning down, I brush my lips across hers. Sparks shoot to every nerve ending as her breath hitches.

"Thank you," I whisper.

I entwine her fingers with mine and turn us toward the kitchen entry.

I've thought the last few days about how I want to spend our time together. While the temptation to go out into the city is strong, I can't help feeling a selfish desire to keep ourselves locked away from the outside. Our time together is precious. I want to keep her all to myself.

"I thought we could stay here for today?" I suggest, hopeful she feels the same. "But, if you prefer, we could go out."

"Staying here sounds perfect. I like it just being us today."

Her response calms my worry and shows despite my insecurity she is just as protective of our time.

I spend part of the morning playing for her because she loves it so much. The pieces I select are beautiful and melodic. I've played them on hundreds of occasions, but today it's like I'm hearing them for the first time.

Once I'm done, we select a movie to watch and nibble on some snacks. On the couch, she sits between my legs, leaning against me with her hand on my chest over my heart. My arm wraps possessively around her hip. We end up dozing off for a brief time before the show ends, lulled by our matched breathing and joined body heat.

Gina is still sleeping as I wake up. Reluctant to end this dream, I look into the face of the woman I am growing to love. The peace she brings me is something I've never experienced. And the hole I've often felt after my parents' deaths fills from the moment she enters the room or when I see her smile.

I move my fingers by her face to brush a few stray wisps of hair behind her ear and then kiss her forehead.

"Wake up, sleeping beauty," I whisper.

Her eyelids flutter open to show deep pools of warm mocha.

"Hi," she says. Her voice is soft from sleep.

Between us, my stomach chooses that moment to rumble its displeasure.

"Um, I think we missed lunch. Are you hungry?"

With a chuckle, she admits, "I could eat." She unfolds her legs and pushes off the couch and turns toward me. She reaches a hand out to me. "Shall we?"

I gladly take it. As I stand, I pull her in for a kiss. Her lips are warm and taste sweet like sugar. They tempt me to skip the food and instead feast on Gina. I know I could sample every inch of her and never be satisfied.

After a moment of indulgence, I move us into the kitchen to rummage through the refrigerator. My uncle has groceries delivered regularly, so there are plenty of choices available.

We decide on a simple meal of roasted chicken and salad greens with dressing, along with fresh fruit.

During dinner, we talk more about our mutual love of music. I found out in our early conversations she's fairly famous in her own right. Gina also tells me stories about all the places she's visited because of her performances. She hints at her father's success and influence making it possible for her to savor the luxury of playing for the joy of it rather than it being a necessity or job. However, she never divulges any specifics of what her father does, which leaves me curious. I envy the freedom she enjoys.

Chapter 9

Once we've finished with our food, we clean the mess in the kitchen in a companionable silence. I steal glances at her often, trying to figure out how the rest of our evening might go. I know I would like nothing more than to feel Gina's skin against mine. The thought sends heat streaking through me. But, I'm anxious about whether she feels ready to take such an intimate step. We've barely known each other a month and mostly only within the confines of the penthouse walls.

After drying the last dish, Gina hangs the towel she's been using. She crosses to the windows and shifts on her feet. I notice she fidgets and plucks at her skirt. Her movements echo the anxiousness and anticipation I feel.

I move behind her, careful not to crowd her personal space. The last thing I want to do is increase her anxiety.

Her eyes meet mine in the reflection. Gently, I grip her shoulder, turning her to face me. I put my finger below her chin, persuading her gaze to lift to mine.

"What is it?"

"I didn't bring a birthday gift for you."

Stunned at her thoughtfulness, I tell her, "Don't you realize you already did?" At her confused expression, I continue. "You are my gift, Regina. You are everything I need."

The color and smile that bloom on her face could brighten a cloud-filled day.

She reaches to her hair and removes the clip holding it in place. Her dark waves tumble down in a cascade of silky strands. Then, she turns back away from me while she sweeps the tresses aside, exposing her neck and shoulders.

Looking at me in the glass, she asks, "Will you help me with the zipper?"

My heart pounds within my ribs for several beats before my fingers find the slider and pull downward in slow motion. Once I've reached the bottom, the back of her dress spreads open and allows the fabric to slip over her curves. It pools at her feet on the floor.

Gina stands in a scrap of black lace and nothing else. The roundness of her backside is on full display before me while the reflection of her body is visible in the tinted glass in front of us. It's the best of both worlds to see all of her at once, but I want to look into her eyes. I want to see the same burning desire I have mirrored in her gaze and to know it's not an illusion. I want to know what I'm feeling is real.

"Will you turn around?"

She grants my wish and circles toward me once more. Her dusty nipples pebble, prompting my mouth to water in anticipation of a taste.

I reach out to brush my thumb over the nub. The contact causes her chin to lift and her breath to hitch, which pushes her breast closer for more contact. I notice the slightest tension of her thighs squeezing together. My cock swells in response. The pressure causes it to strain against my shorts to reach her, to reach paradise.

"You are exquisite."

Her whimper accompanies the rapid pulse in her neck and shallow breaths.

Sliding my palms to the sides of her breasts, I pull her toward me for a searing kiss. My tongue probes for entrance between her lips, which she grants and meets with eager thrusts of her own. When she rises on her tiptoes, I lift her to meld her body against mine. She wraps her legs around my hips causing the heat of her core to build an inferno right where I need her most.

With quick strides, I pivot and direct us to my bedroom. I lay her carefully on the duvet without breaking our connection. Then, I settle my weight over her increasing the contact between us.

I feel her hands reach over my shoulders to work the shirt up my back. A second later, it's over my head and tossed on the floor from my lustful impatience. Our lips crash together once again in a ravaging kiss.

Her delicate fingers then slip between us to the waistband of my shorts.

She breaks her mouth away from mine and groans. "Off!"

Lifting myself off the bed, I shed the rest of my clothing. She shimmies out of her panties at the same time. Our eyes never break their connection.

I crawl back to her, taking a moment to pause.

"Are you sure, Gina?"

"I've never been more sure of anything." Her tone is full of conviction and desire.

We haven't talked about it, but I'm certain she's a virgin, just like me.

"I don't have any protection for us to use. It hasn't exactly been a consideration for me."

"It's fine," she assures me. "I'm on the pill. And there's been no one before you. I don't want anything between us, anyway. I just want to feel."

The thought of feeling her surround me completely with no barrier sends my craving for her into overdrive. I can't imagine a more perfect moment between us.

"Please, Zel, I need you."

This time when my mouth finds hers, it's slow and consuming as I pour everything I feel into our kiss. She answers with the same unhurried intensity.

The shifting of our bodies has the head of my cock positioned at her entrance. When I push in, I think my entire body might combust into flames. The sensation is unlike anything I've ever experienced. A rush of heat floods over every nerve ending.

Gina breaks our lips apart with heavy breaths. Her brows pinch together slightly. Concerned I'm hurting her, I pull back, despite the temptation to bury myself deep inside her.

"No! Don't go anywhere," she pants.

"I don't want to hurt you."

"I'll be okay. It'll only be a moment."

"We'll go slowly," I promise.

She nods her agreement with cheeks flushed and eyes lit with desire.

I slide back into the position I left. It's likely only a hair's width of movement, but from the buzzing sensation throughout my body I'd swear my cock slid all the way home. Our moans are simultaneous.

Instinct spurs me to taste the ambrosia of her skin on display in front of me. I circle one nipple with my tongue, then the next. With each lick, Gina's back arches higher, pushing me deeper into her.

Hoping to distract her fully, I suck the bud into my mouth. Then, I scrape my teeth across it, careful not to bite down, before my tongue soothes away any sting. The action makes her cry out with pleasure. As she bucks in response, the movement has us almost joined.

I repeat the process on the other side, but this time hollow out my cheeks to increase the suction. The next moment I'm inside her as deep as I can go, stars winking behind my eyes.

Feeling her walls contract around me, I don't know how I'll keep from erupting.

"Oh, my god." Moving her head from side to side, she moans, "Move. Please, move. You have to move, Zel!"

The slide out is excruciatingly good. I pull out all the way to the tip before I begin the push back into her body. It feels better with each stroke and even more so as my speed increases.

Sweat beads on my forehead from the control I feel is about to slip. The droplets land onto her chest, marking her.

Gina angles her hips to meet me thrust for thrust. The friction is heaven and hell combined.

When ripples vibrate in her core, her gaze holds mine. I watch in fascination as she falls apart and an expression of pure bliss forms on her beautiful face. It's only a moment longer before my climax roars through and overtakes me. When everything pours out of me, I experience the strongest feeling of euphoria I've ever known.

Before I collapse on top of her, I lower myself and roll us to our sides, bodies still entwined. The thought of separating from her creates a physical ache making me pull her closer. She was born to be mine.

The tug of sleep is strong as my eyes grow heavy. But before I can be pulled under completely, I speak the words I've been waiting days to say right as oblivion descends.

"I love you, Regina Prince."

Chapter 10

The warmth of Gina's body next to mine radiates through me while soft lips flutter along my neck. All the sensations bring me out of the richest sleep I've had in years.

My eyes slowly open to a darkened room, lit only by the illumination of the city outside.

I turn my head and see a glow to Gina's skin. Rolling into her, I bury my nose in her hair and relish the fragrance I crave. My lips gently suck the sensitive dip between her neck and collarbone. She sighs in appreciation. The simple sound awakens all of my desire again. She giggles and then moans as I push my leg between hers.

"We never had dessert," she says.

"Oh, I believe we did."

She playfully swats at my shoulder and leans back to look into my face.

"I meant the cupcake I brought you. You know, for your birthday?"

"Hmm, that dessert. I'm sure you taste better."

"You have not celebrated until you eat birthday cake. And it needs to happen *on* your birthday or it doesn't count."

I smile at her insistence. "Well, I guess we should go have some then."

She disentangles from me. She looks giddy over the prospect of sugar and chocolate.

Gina walks with confidence around the bed as the glow of the moon and city lights glisten across her skin. She bends to grab my discarded shirt and pulls it over her body, but not before my gaze devours every inch of her.

She turns with expectation clear on her face.

"Come on, lazy!"

Chuckling at her impatience, I rise from the bed and stride to the dresser. My cock juts out and twitches when I hear her light hum of appreciation from near the edge of the room.

In search of some shorts, I find what I need and slide them up to hang just over my hips. Then, I meet her at the doorway, putting my hand in hers.

When we enter the kitchen, she takes a seat on the high stool. I stand close while she removes the cupcake from its transparent box. A smear of frosting coats the side of her thumb from the task. She licks if off without paying attention to the effect her action has on me. As my gaze focuses on the stroke of her tongue, I envision her doing the same to me. The mental image makes my cock swell. I'm torn between fulfilling her request for the dessert and carrying her back to my bed.

With a push in my direction, the confection is in front of me. Then she says, "I don't have a candle, but you still need to make a wish. Birthday wishes are powerful."

Not wanting to hurt her feelings by ignoring her sweet gesture, I think about everything I would have wished for a month ago. All the things I thought weren't even possible. Then, I consider what I have sitting before me and know nothing I could ever imagine can compare.

"There's nothing to wish for. I have everything I want," I admit.

Despite the low light, the flush on her cheeks is easy to see.

"Then, I'll make your wish."

"Is that even allowed? I don't think it works that way."

She shrugs, showing her determination to make up her own rules. "If you say it is, why not?"

"Okay, you make my birthday wish."

I watch as she closes her eyes and bites her bottom lip in concentration. Her mouth moves like she's forming the words for her request, but no sound comes out. When she stops, she takes a deep breath, opens her eyes, and then smiles at me.

"Done! Now, eat the cake or it won't come true."

"Only if we share. I insist."

Gina reaches for a knife in the butcher block on the counter. She cuts the sweet treat into bite-sized pieces and lifts one to my mouth. I dutifully open to accept her offering. We spend the next few minutes feeding each other the delectable morsels, never breaking our heated stare.

Once she's given me the last bite, I sweep my finger over the casing, gathering the leftover frosting. I want the feeling of her mouth on me. As my hand hovers before her, she wraps her lips around my finger and sucks, sliding to the end. It's better than I imagined. The erotic display sends my lust into overdrive. The only coherent thought in my head comes out of my mouth.

"I wonder if you taste as good."

Her eyes widen in anticipation as she watches me drop to my knees. I lift my shirt off of her thighs, exposing the heaven I want. She leans back to brace against the countertop edge and spreads her knees wide, giving me better access. Crowding into the space, I push her open even more before I move her legs over my shoulders. The motion brings my mouth to the perfect position for indulgence.

I look up to note the vision of her vulnerability on display. She shifts the control over to me with no hesitation.

Her eyes are glassy with desire while her chest rises and falls with rapid breaths. Keeping our gaze locked, I swipe my tongue up to savor the first taste of her.

"Mmm, so good," I confirm.

Her sigh is pure contentment as her head falls back.

I lap at her sweet flavor until her pants become fervent cries. Even as her thighs tighten around my ears, I don't stop until she is limp and spent from the powerful release.

Rising to my feet, I lick my lips while satisfaction flows through me. I kiss her lips lightly before I lift her into my arms and carry her to my room.

Once I place her on the edge of the bed, she pulls me close. I am then standing in front of her, a captive to the desire in her eyes. I am at her mercy as my cock is perfectly aligned with her seductive mouth.

Her hands smooth up to the waistband of my shorts and pull them down to free my rigid length.

With my crooked finger beneath her chin, I persuade her to look at me.

"You don't have to."

Her eyes glitter like diamonds, burning with lust.

"Oh, I do. I can't help myself."

The moment the last syllable ends, the end of her tongue slips out to lick the pearl seeping from my tip. Next, her mouth covers the head. I sway on my feet and place my hands on her shoulders for balance, spreading my feet wide. I'm not sure how I'll stay on my feet.

Gina scoots forward to the edge of the mattress while sliding her lips down as far as they will go. Just when I think she can't take anymore of me, her hands grip my ass to pull me in until my cock connects with the back of her throat. The fit of her mouth over me is perfection.

While I pull out slowly, at a speed I think might kill me from pleasure, she hums. The vibration travels through every nerve ending in my body, and then fuses together at the base of my spine. Before I can leave the heat of her mouth, she pulls me back in and watches me the entire time. It's by far the most erotic scene I can imagine, etched in my mind forever.

She continues to work at a steady rhythm, determined to take her time in the task. It's torturous pleasure.

My fingers weave into her hair to apply the smallest amount of pressure in hopes she'll take pity on me before I collapse into a puddle at her feet.

Gina must sense my need building as my hands hold her head steady. She lets me take control, allowing me to stroke in and out of her mouth. My tempo is faster and falters the closer I get to the climax. When I move to pull out for my release, she counters by locking my hips in place with her arms. She takes me as deep as she can. That action is the catalyst causing me to explode into her throat. She swallows down everything I have to give, leaving me weak and delirious from the high.

Barely able to stand on my feet, I stagger a step backward to slide free from her lips. She takes my hand to pull me into the bed and molds her body to mine.

Sighing with contentment, she tells me, "I love you, too, Zel."

Even though the ecstasy I feel in my body is from my release, the burst of emotion in my chest has everything to do with her words. Nothing can compare to it.

We fall asleep bonded together in body and heart. And for the first time, I'm grateful to live in this glass tower.

Chapter 11

Something rouses me from sleep.

I look at the doorway, blinking it into focus. There's nothing, no image or shadow. Not that there should be.

Glancing at Gina, she's curled next to me. Her expression is soft and content in slumber. I'm mesmerized by her beauty.

Just as I close my eyes to doze off again, a door slams. The sound jars me and stops my heart.

"Gina," I whisper, panic lacing my words. "Wake up." I shake her shoulder without taking my eyes off the door.

"What is it? What's wrong?"

"Well, I don't care what the damn papers say. Find a loophole!" My uncle's voice booms through the apartment. The fury in his tone is worse than I've ever heard it.

He shouldn't be here. He said his plans were for the weekend. Then, I remember Gina shouldn't be here either. The flow of blood freezes in my veins while fear seizes me.

I listen as his footsteps echo on the marble floor. The volume of his steps lessens, a sign he's moving away from my room. I assume that means he's going to his office.

I leap into action the moment the sound of footsteps fade. I grab anything of Gina's off the floor. After tossing them on the bed, I pull on my shorts.

"Quick, get up. That was my uncle. Get dressed."

"Zel, what's he doing here? What're we going to do?"

"I'm getting you out of here!"

Once she's clothed with her shoes in her grasp, she follows behind me to the bedroom door. I lean out to peer around the frame. A narrow stream of yellow light shines from the other side of the living room. The source is my uncle's desk lamp. He must have the door partially closed. I can hear his voice. His tone is cruel, but the words are hard to understand.

I have to sneak Gina out before he catches us. Now is the best chance we have.

With her hand tight in mine, I gather her close to my back, prepared to dart across the open space into the kitchen. Moving as one, our feet barely make any sound as we rush past the couch. My eyes are on the cracked office door the entire time.

I think we're in the clear when I hear my uncle's raised voice again.

"I don't care what it takes," he growls. "I won't hand everything over just because some paper says that punk is finally old enough. That money is mine!"

My feet become rooted in place. The fury in his voice resonates through the space.

"I haven't spent the last ten years being saddled to my sister's kid to wind up with nothing. Fix this! Now!"

A fog of questions clutters my mind.

"Zel, what's he talking about?" Gina whispers. "Zel!" She yanks on my arm jolting me from my trance.

"I-I don't know." My voice sounds wooden and hollow to my own ears. Everything feels like slow motion under water. Explanations hover just beyond the edge of understanding.

Suddenly, I'm slammed with the realization we're still standing exposed in the open room. With an insistent nudge on her shoulders, I steer Gina toward the service elevator. I keep an ear out for footsteps while she slips through the kitchen door.

She pushes the button to call for the elevator, and then runs back to me.

"I'll come back tomorrow," she insists.

"No, you can't. I don't know if he'll be here. I won't risk it."

Her lips brush over mine in a firm, yet quick kiss. Then, she presses her palm on my chest to move me out of the opening. She closes the door with a soft click before the chime announces the elevator.

A lump forms in my throat at the thought of not knowing when I might see Gina again.

As I turn to go back to my room, the light in the apartment brightens. My uncle's office door opens as he exits. I duck beside the refrigerator in hopes he won't come in my direction. My pulse takes off in a sprint.

Peeking out from my hiding place, I see him immersed in his tablet while he walks to his room opposite from me. I take a deep breath before I notice the remains of the packaging from my birthday cupcake. When he's stepped into his room, I quickly gather up the trash and dispose of it all in the bin under the last few days of takeout containers.

Then, on shaky feet, I dash to my room and dive back into bed. The blood rushes to my head while the erratic beats of my heart pound in my chest. The adrenaline pouring through my system makes it difficult to breathe.

When I hear my uncle's steps nearing my doorway, my body turns to stone. A cold sweat covers my brow as I wonder if he heard me.

Through the slits of my lids, I watch as he lingers there, never crossing the threshold. His figure looms like a harbinger of misery. I expect him to wake me like he's often done over the years, but he doesn't. After several seconds that drag on for longer than I would like, he spins away. Once another door slams, the pent up breath I've held in my throat releases in a whoosh and leaves me gasping for air.

I don't know what's going on, but my gut tells me it's nothing good. It's time for me to figure out how to leave and quickly. I just hope somehow I'll be able to see Gina or let her know.

Chapter 12

It's moving into the second day since I snuck Gina out of the apartment. Too many hours from the last time I felt her soft lips on mine, held her in my arms, or even saw her face. I ache to hold her again. My heart burns without her.

I have no way of knowing if she's okay or when she might come back. She said she would, but I told her to stay away. I'm worried if she does return what might happen, especially if she shows up when I'm gone. But, even worse, I'm tormented by the thought Gina will listen to what I said and not come back at all.

Another bothersome issue is my uncle has become unpredictable. I never know when he'll leave or return or how long he'll be gone. It makes the situation difficult to find the best opportunity to leave.

The change in his behavior has me on edge. His temper has been shorter than normal and nonexistent when he deems it necessary to speak to me. I know he's hiding something important. I fear the outcome when I find out what it is.

I spend my time immersed in my music while I wait because I don't know what else to do. This only increases my melancholy and causes me to miss Gina more.

When my fingers cramp from hours of playing, I finally stop. I trudge to my room to stare out the windows of my glass tower, wishing I was anywhere else except here.

My uncle returned home an hour ago and closed himself in his office. I've heard heated conversations, at least from his end, all day, but couldn't make out the exact words through the heavy door.

By late evening, I hear him emerge. His staccato footsteps click on the floor.

"Yes. Fine. I'll be there in less than fifteen minutes," he growls.

As I rise off the bed to watch him from the door frame, I see him end the call and punctuate it with a curse. He leaves the apartment without a glance or word in my direction.

In the few moments of reprieve I have, I sit on the couch and follow the sun as it lowers behind the skyscrapers of the city. Shafts of light from the sunset stream through the spaces between the concrete, steel, and glass. I gaze out until the colors of the sky have turned deep shades of purple and blue to leave very little light in the room.

When I rise from the couch and turn toward my room, I notice the smallest beam of lamplight spilling from a slit in the office door. It shouldn't be there. My uncle never leaves the door open or unlocked when he's not around.

The pull of temptation and curiosity move my feet forward. Maybe I can find some answers. With a push on the door, it swings wide.

Boxes are open on the floor. Their lids off and tossed aside. The contents are in disarray and spilling out of the boxes. Unorganized piles and papers are all over an enormous mahogany desk, which draw me to them.

I sift through the documents, recognizing nothing, until my name jumps off a page midway through the stack. It seems like some kind of contract.

I read over paragraphs of clauses and legal phrasing. After flipping past several sheets, there are sections listing my uncle's name, percentages of control, and sizeable dollar amounts. The last page shows his signature, along with another person named as an executive at a music studio. The date on the paper is one year after my parents' deaths.

Attached are more typed pages. These identify a conservatorship in bold print on the front. As I read, phrases like *estate of the minor child*, *age of twenty-one*, and *signatures required* etch into my memory.

"You shouldn't be in here."

My uncle's voice startles me. Ice slides through my veins at his venomous tone. I'd been so distracted with reading, I never heard him come into the apartment or the office.

"What is this?" I demand as I shake the papers in my hand. Not that I expect him to tell me.

To my surprise, he does.

"Oh, that's just the control I have over your life. Or more importantly, the money."

"What money?"

"The money left to you, along with your royalties. You see as your guardian and manager, I decide everything. I have access to everything."

"How is that possible? And how didn't I know?"

"Well, you see, nephew, that's how your mother set it up. At least the guardian part. The manager's job was my doing. You were a child when your parents died and in no position to provide for yourself. She knew if something ever happened to them, someone had to take the job. Guess she thought I was a decent choice."

My mind jumps to a horrible conclusion.

"You killed them?" I feel rage pulsing at my temples. My hands ball into fists.

"Oh, no. Their accident was just lucky. For me, that is." A hollow, maniacal laugh follows his sinister words. Then, his expression contorts into something dark and evil. "But, then I find out my bitch of a sister tried to screw me out of everything. Expected me to just sign and hand it all over to *you* like some doting uncle and walk away after having to be responsible for you for so many years!"

Everything clicks into place. All the hours he spent hounding me over practices, the recording studio on the same floor, the micromanaging of my time, and the restrictions he kept over me. It was always about his greed and the money.

"Just take it. I don't want it."

"See? It doesn't work that way." As his head moves from side to side, he laughs, but it holds no amusement. Then, he continues, "I can't take it. It's your money. If I want the money, I have to keep you around. How unfortunate for me." He pulls a pistol from behind his back and points it directly at me. "But, I don't have to like it or really look at you ever again," he sneers.

With a twitch of the gun barrel to the left, he directs me to move around the desk.

I walk slowly, worried what might set him further on edge. I don't want him to consider an option where I'm not breathing. I berate myself for ever wanting a connection with this man. My stomach rolls at the thought that he's related to the mother I remember.

As I approach him, his cellphone rings. He thrusts the gun forward, prompting me to stop a few feet from him.

While he keeps his shrewd gaze locked on me, he answers the call, "Yeah?" He waits a beat before he responds. "No! I said the movers need to be here before noon tomorrow. If they can't, someone else will earn triple the fee." He forces the phone back into his pocket, never taking his eyes off me.

"Movers?"

"Yes. I've decided there's too many nosy people around here. We will be somewhere no one can question me again. Let's go, dear nephew of mine."

He takes a step forward and yanks on my arm to propel me into the living room. My thoughts spin out of control as I realize if he takes me from this building I will see no one ever again. Gina will never know where I am if she returns.

Out of desperation, I try one last time to convince him he doesn't need me.

Slowing my feet to buy time, I beg, "Just tell me what to sign. I'll do it. You can take it all and leave me here."

"A nice thought, really. I wish it were that simple."

Frustration buzzes under my skin. I just want him gone. "Go! Live your life," I shout.

"I plan to, but first, you're too much of a distraction. You need to take a nice long rest."

Before I can turn around to question what he means, a force hits me hard on the back of the head. I crumple in a heap on the floor. The last thing I remember as my eyes close is the cold marble on my cheek while a burning fire of pain runs over my scalp.

Chapter 13

When I wake up, daylight has already crept over the buildings of the city. I don't know how long I've been unconscious, but I have a general idea. Part of me still wishes I was, based on the intense throbbing in my head.

Rolling with ease to the side of the bed, I sit and wait for a wave of nausea to pass. When I think I can stand, I push to my feet. The room warps in front of my eyes as I sway.

I make it to the door, only to find it locked from the outside. Somehow, I'm not surprised.

From what I can tell, the apartment on the other side is silent. I figure there isn't any point in yelling. No one will hear me, other than my uncle, if he's even here. That was part of the appeal he said, so no one could hear my playing.

The fogginess in my head and jackhammer between my ears force me to lie back down. I don't know if I've fallen asleep again or am daydreaming when there's a whisper from the door.

"Zel!" The familiar sweet voice floats through the frame.

My shock has me carefully rising from the bed to move toward the door.

"Gina?"

"Zel, are you there?"

"What are you doing here?"

"I told you I'd be back. I came back for you."

I'm torn between elation and frustration she's here, along with fear she'll get caught. The fear takes priority. I can't let her put her safety in jeopardy over me.

"Gina, you need to leave. If my uncle finds you..."

As if my words summoned him, I hear his voice.

"Well, who do we have here?"

"You need to let Zel go. Now," she commands.

Her voice is strong and fierce. I can picture the fire in her eyes as she faces him. If I wasn't so terrified for her, I'd feel desire course through me from the image.

"No, my dear. I don't think I do. It's none of your concern. You should be the one leaving. Although, I don't think that's possible now."

I don't understand what's happening on the other side of the door. I'm terrified Gina's in danger. There's shuffling and the sounds of items being knocked over when I hear her scream.

"Gina!"

I'm frantic to escape and get out of my room in any way possible. I bang on the wood with my fists. Frantic it's not enough, I look around the room. I see the desk chair and grab it. Then, I use it to make the loudest noise possible.

In between the strikes against the door, Gina's voice comes through again.

"Zel! Stop!"

"Gina?" I'm not sure I really believe it's her.

"Move away from the door."

I step back, still holding the chair.

As the door swings wide, I see her standing there more beautiful than ever. She smiles when she sees me.

"Are you okay?"

"Me?" I ask in confusion. "He locked me in a room. You were out there with *him*."

She laughs. "Yes, well, that wasn't much fun. But, it's fine now. Are you coming out?"

My feet, rooted in place a moment ago, sprint to her. My arms gather her close as I bury my nose in her hair to breathe in the scent I've missed. I hang onto her for dear life. In return, she clings to me just as hard.

A deep masculine cough interrupts our moment. "Regina?"

She sighs. It's filled with equal parts contentment and annoyance as she angles her face to look at me without unwrapping her arms from my waist.

"Zel, I'd like to introduce my father, Samuel Prince." She nods toward a tall, distinguished gentleman with a striking resemblance to her. "Dad, this is Zel Thatcher."

"Mr. Thatcher, it's a pleasure to finally meet you. Regina has told me a lot about you."

"Um, sorry, sir. I wish I could say the same, but she hasn't spoken much about you at all. It's still nice to meet you though."

He laughs lightly. "I can't say I'm surprised. She usually doesn't talk about me. I suppose I should feel honored she mentioned anything about me to you. Some people might think it's because I'm her parent and I'd embarrass her. But, I know it's because she so independent."

I look into Gina's face as she playfully rolls her eyes at his comment.

Arching my brow, I ask a silent question.

"My dad is a music producer. He also owns a major recording studio. So, he's kind of well-known."

I can tell she tries to play it off, but her admiration of him seeps through her words.

"Don't worry, Zel. I don't take her act of indifference personally," he tells me. "She just does it to prove she can do everything on her own, which is fine by me. It means she values what she works for."

Her lips twitch in response. A smile barely contained.

The shock of the situation finally begins to subside, which makes me look around the apartment. I notice the front door is open with a man standing, his back to me, inside the threshold. If I had to guess based on his size, lack of movement, and the imposing wall he imitates, he's some kind of security. I am also keenly aware my uncle is nowhere in the apartment. Gina picks up on my confusion.

"Gone," she states.

Her father elaborates when I turn my stare to him. "Your uncle is in custody with the authorities. He has a lot of explaining and answers to give. He'll likely be spending a lot of time in prison for kidnapping, fraud, and embezzlement. Those are only some of the charges he faces."

As the flow of adrenaline drains out of my body, it becomes more difficult to stay on my feet. The ache in my skull also returns. Gina feels me slump and helps to hold me up. She guides me to the couch.

Once seated, I respond, "I'm not sure I understand all of that, but the kidnapping I get."

She sits next to me and grips my hand. Before telling me more, she glances at her dad, who nods at her to continue.

"It turns out that your uncle has been in control of your estate since your parents died. Not all that unusual since he became your guardian. It might have been fine at first. But, somewhere along the way, he realized your talent could make him even more money. Then, he learned that although he was to handle everything when you were growing up, all of that stopped on your twenty-first birthday with a simple signature from you."

"I never knew there was an estate of any kind. Or any money from my music."

"I think he planned to keep it that way," she says in frustration. "I would guess he enjoyed a certain lifestyle thanks to you and didn't want to give it up."

"Power and money change people, Zel. Some for the better and some not," Mr. Prince adds. "But, by the looks of things, you won't have to worry about him again."

It's a relief to know I'm no longer trapped in my life, but then a reality sets in for the first time.

"Zel, what is it?"

"I'm not sure what to do now. He's my only family. And this is the only place I've lived for so long. Now, I really am alone."

While the thought of finally being free is enticing, it also creates a certain panic of the unknown. To suddenly go from having no choice in anything to having all of them is daunting.

With her palms on my face, Gina turns me to look at her. The warmth shining in her eyes brings the familiar ache to my chest.

"You are not alone. Never again. You have me."

The brush of her lips on mine sends electric currents coursing through me. The kiss is brief and soft, but intimate. The desire I see burning in her gaze pulls me in and washes away all of my sorrows and doubts. My heart recognizes the melody inside her and sings for her in return.

Lost in each other, I barely hear her father excuse himself, saying he'll be right outside whenever we are ready to leave.

"So, Zel Thatcher, you have a choice to make. The first in an endless list it seems."

"What's that?"

"Well, you need to decide if you're staying to live in this apartment or not."

I look around the place that has been my residence for a decade. It's expensive and stylish with an exquisite view of the city. But, while I have spent almost every moment here, there are no feelings of joy or comfort in the space. It's never been a home. And I can't imagine any place I want to leave more.

When my eyes return to her, the smile that blooms on my face is born from happiness.

With my heart full of love and hope, I tell her, "My home is wherever you are."

Beams of joy radiate from her eyes. She stands, offering me her hand.

"Then, let's get out of here and find a place just for us."

Taking her hand in mine, I join her to walk out of my glass tower together, leaving it behind forever.

Chapter 14

Six months later

As I walk down the busy city street of Corona, I see my name on a digital billboard high above me. But, this time there's a picture of me with the scrolling letters. It's all surreal. The freedom I have, being recognized, the pleasant chaos of my life now, and the peace I feel.

Months ago, I never imagined the possibility that I would step out of my home and have people want to meet me. Or even crazier, they would want to have my autograph and take pictures with me.

I also didn't think I would find my passion for music again. That is until Gina knocked on my door. She is the miracle that made it happen. She is the reason everything has become a reality. And what's even better is the love I found with her.

Since the day the authorities arrested and set charges for my uncle, he's been awaiting trial for all the horrible things he's done. I haven't visited him, nor do I feel sorry for him. He made his bed.

I found out my parents' attorney kept copies of all the documents, especially those regarding the conservatorship of the estate. He had been trying to reach me, which is what sent my uncle into a frenzy and everything in to motion. The lawyer also had a birth certificate to prove my identity and age, along with my uncle's previous agreement to the terms. So, with a signature of my own and a filing with the court, everything became rightfully mine as was my mother's wish.

I sold the penthouse apartment without regret. I couldn't see myself living there again after being confined in it for so many years. I talked it over with Gina, but she assured me whatever I decided she would support. My gut told me despite the beautiful memories she and I shared there, she didn't want to step foot in that glass prison ever again, anyway.

After the sale of the penthouse, Gina's father offered for me to stay with them until I settled everything from my uncle's mess. I declined however because I didn't feel it was appropriate. Plus, I wanted to take some time for myself, even though the desire to be near Gina all the time was ever present. I ended up finding a small, temporary bungalow close to her and her father's residence.

It all worked out perfectly because I was also lucky enough to find the perfect place for Gina and I to start our lives together. If all goes well today, I won't ever have to worry about her not being by my side again.

So now, I'm looking forward to my future. It's a future that includes Regina Prince forever.

I make my way through the streets to the lake where we had our first date. Excitement bubbles in me, accompanied by the burning desire to have Gina in my arms. I haven't seen her for a few days in order for me to prepare what I have planned. I also have a surprise or two up my sleeve she won't expect.

As I enter the park, I see Gina waiting for me on the bridge. She is a vision, dressed in turquoise. Her deep brunette hair falls in loose waves and moves with the breeze. I will never tire of looking at her.

She hears me approach and turns in my direction. At first, her eyes widen in shock when she sees me and then her smile brightens. The sparkle of love in her eyes causes my knees to go weak. I can't believe she picked me.

"Hi."

I immediately take her hand in mine to pull her close and brush my lips across hers. The blush on her cheeks mirrors the flash of heat racing through my body.

"Hi yourself," she coos. "You had your hair cut."

"Yeah," I pause. "Do you mind?"

"No, I like it. I think it's a handsome choice." She giggles, then says, "Besides, it's not like your hair had magical powers."

A laugh bubbles out of my throat. "Wouldn't that be something?"

She brushes her fingers through the much shorter strands, mesmerized by the change. My scalp tingles from her touch. I could stand here all day and be content, but I have a plan.

Pulling myself out of the spell she puts me under, I ask, "Would you like to walk?"

"Sure," she agrees. "Where to?"

I shrug to try and not give anything away. "Let's just stroll a bit."

Her delicate brow arches in question, but she doesn't say a word. I'm sure she can tell I'm up to something. And yet, she smiles sweetly and looks up at me in anticipation. She wraps her arm through mine and waits for me to lead her in the direction I want us to go.

My feet propel us to a spot I found months ago, tucked away on the side of the lake. As soon as I saw it, I knew this was the place for us. I also realized at the same time I needed Gina in my life forever.

We walk closer as a quaint cottage stands surrounded by color comes into view. Flowers bloom where the dying brush was once covering it. Fresh paint gave the siding of the house and the fence a much needed face-lift. An archway covered in ivy welcomes us at the end of the walkway. The most notable change is the 'for sale' sign holding a 'sold' banner across the front in bright red lettering.

"Oh, Zel, look at this! This place is so beautiful! I love it." Her voice holds a fair amount of disappointment.

"If you think it looks so nice, why do you sound so sad?"

"Well, it looks like someone has bought the place. It probably sounds silly, but I can just picture it being ours."

Lifting her chin with my finger, I assure her, "It doesn't sound silly at all. It sounds perfect in fact."

I can't deny the urge to kiss her. As my lips seal with hers, our bodies fit together. Her sigh is full of promise.

When I pull away, her eyes remain closed, giving me a chance to pull the key ring from my pocket.

Gina blinks against the bright sunlight to see it dangling in front of her.

First, I watch as a confused expression forms on her beautiful face. Then finally, comprehension dawns as her hand shakes while reaching to take the key ring from me. Before her fingers close around it, she sees the canary yellow diamond solitaire nestled beside the house key.

"Zel?" The hopefulness in her tone and expression stirs the butterflies inside me.

"This is the place I want to start a new life. Our life. If you'll have me."

"If I'll have you?" Tears shimmer in her eyes through the joy I see.

Lowering onto one knee, I gaze into the face of the woman who saved me. She saved me from a life of loneliness and isolation, but she also restored my passion for music.

"Regina Prince, there is no one else for me other than you. You stole my heart the moment I saw you on the sidewalk outside that glass tower. I didn't know it then, but you were meant to free me. But, in return, you've cast me under your spell to remain yours forever."

She giggles at my statement.

I take the key ring from her hand. Despite my tremors that make the two items clink together, I pull the diamond off carefully. I hold the platinum band to hover in front of her ring finger.

"Gina, I'll love you for the rest of my life. Will you marry me?"

"Yes," she exclaims.

I slide the band onto her finger and then rise, scooping her into my arms. As I lower her to her feet again, she peppers my face with kisses before giving me a last one full of promise, desire, and love.

When she's finished, she holds her hand up in the sunlight to admire the ring.

"The yellow is so beautiful!"

"It reminds me of the yellow dress you wore on our first date here. You took my breath away you were so beautiful."

She smiles at me and asks, "Zel, is all of this real?"

"Yes," I assure her, "but it's also our very own fairy tale."

Acknowledgments

I have to start my acknowledgments by thanking all of the readers who purchase and open my books to read. Without you, I wouldn't be able to keep writing and doing what I love. So, thank you. I hope you enjoy every story I write.

I have to thank a dear writer friend, Pascale, for her invitation to write this story and have it be a part of an anthology. She was so sweet to think of me and give me this opportunity to join such an incredible group of authors. This story was written during one of the most difficult times of my life. Her belief in me and patience pushed me to complete it and I will be forever grateful for her support.

Next is my tribe. These women (along with so many others) are my foundation. They support me, nudge me, and even kick me in the backside when I need it. They are always available when I need them for plotting, writer's block, proofing, and when I've reached my limit of characters not doing what I want. Thank you, from the bottom of my heart, to Dee, Shelley, and Jen. I can't express how much all of you mean to me.

For my biggest, loudest, and best cheerleader I could ever ask for, Diana. You have been with me on this journey of mine from almost the very beginning. My life is so much fuller with you in it. We have laughed together, cried together, and celebrated together. You help me in so many ways and are a constant source of support. Thank you for all you do to help me stay sane. I love you.

Lastly, for my family, thank you for believing in me, for cheering me on when I doubted myself, for reminding me that I can do anything. The support I get from you means everything. I hope I make you proud.

About the Author

Emily Gray is a bestselling author of romantic suspense and contemporary romance. Originally from Virginia, she decided she was tired of dealing with cold weather and moved with her family to the Florida sunshine. She's spent her life constantly thinking up stories in her head and finally decided it was time to put them on paper. Her debut novel, The Marine, was published in 2016 as part of her Heroes & Warriors series. All her stories focus on strong, passionate heroes and kick-ass heroines who don't need saving. She's sure to provide them all with the HEAs they deserve once she's thrown in an obstacle or two so her characters realize finding love is worth every struggle they encounter.

Here are all the ways to connect with Emily:

authoremilygray@gmail.com

Facebook profile: www.facebook.com/authoremilygray

Follow her page at www.facebook.com/emilygrayauthor

Reader Group:
https://www.facebook.com/groups/1080748785413753

Bookbub: https://www.bookbub.com/profile/emily-gray

Instagram: https://www.instagram.com/emilygrayauthor

Goodreads:
https://www.goodreads.com/author/show/15171566.Emily
_Gray

www.emilygray.org

More Books by Emily Gray

Heroes & Warriors Series

The Marine, Book 1
The Fighter, Book 2

Protect & Serve Series
(Police and Fire: Operation Alpha)

Shelter for Allegra, Book 1

Coming soon

Heroes & Warriors Series

The Specialist, Book 3

Christmas Springs Series

Christmas Dreams for Eve, Book 1